POKÉMON The Movie 2000

THE POWER OF ONE

Movie Adaptation by
Tracey West

SCHOLASTIC INC.
New York   Toronto   London   Auckland   Sydney
Mexico City   New Delhi   Hong Kong

Special thanks to Norman Grossfeld for his creative input.

ISBN 0-439-19968-9

© 1997-2000 Nintendo, CREATURES, GAME FREAK, TV Tokyo, ShoPro.
© Pikachu Project '99
All rights reserved. Published by Scholastic, Inc.
SCHOLASTIC and associated logos are trademarks and/or registered trademarks of Scholastic Inc.

12 11 10 9 8 7 6 5 4   0 1 2 3 4 5 6/0

Printed in the U.S.A.
First Scholastic printing, July 2000

Pokémon Dictionary

Welcome to the world of Pokémon! To help you enjoy *Pokémon the Movie 2000* (and this book based on the movie), here's a little Poké "cheat sheet." It's all you need to know in a nutshell — or a Poké Ball!

CHARACTERS

Ash Ketchum. On his tenth birthday, Ash became a Pokémon trainer — someone who catches and takes care of Pokémon. Ash's team of Pokémon includes Pidgeot, Muk, Tauros, Lapras, Snorlax, Krabby, Bulbasaur, Charizard, Squirtle, and of course, Pikachu.

Misty. Born in beautiful Cerulean City,

Misty specializes in training Water Pokémon. She travels around with Ash and Brock. Misty takes along Starmie, Staryu, Goldeen, Seadra, and Psyduck.

Pikachu. Ash was shocked when he got this Electric Pokémon the day he became a Pokémon trainer. Now Pikachu is more than just Ash's Pokémon — it's a good friend.

Pokémon. Pokémon are creatures that come in all shapes, sizes, and personalities. Pokémon trainers capture Pokémon and train them to face other Pokémon in battle. Most Pokémon can evolve into more advanced forms of Pokémon by gaining battle experience or by being exposed to special stones. There are at least 151 Pokémon in the world — and trainers are finding new types of Pokémon all the time!

Team Rocket. A trio of Pokémon thieves made up of a teenage girl named Jessie, a teenage boy named James, and their talking Pokémon, Meowth. They're under orders from their boss to steal rare Pokémon — including Pikachu. So far, they haven't had much luck!

Tracey Sketchit. As a Pokémon watcher,

Tracey carefully observes Pokémon behavior. He likes to draw Pokémon in his sketchbook. When he met Ash on the Orange Islands, he decided to join him on his journey to catch more Pokémon. Tracey's role model is Professor Oak, and he hopes to study with the great Pokémon expert one day. He likes to travel with his Pokémon, Marill, Venonat, and Scyther.

TYPES OF POKéMON

While all Pokémon are different, they can be grouped according to several basic types. A Pokémon's type determines what special powers it will have in battle. Some Pokémon are a combination of more than one type.

1. **Bug.** These creepy crawly creatures look like insects — but they're much bigger than the ones you're used to!

2. **Dragon.** They may look like the dragons in fairy tales, but these Pokémon have abilities you've never read about.

3. **Electric.** With thunderbolts and other electric attacks, these Pokémon are shockingly good in battle!

4. **Fighting.** These pumped-up Pokémon pack a powerful punch!

5. **Fire.** These flame-shooting Pokémon are too hot to handle!

6. **Flying.** These Pokémon often have the advantage, because they can attack in midair.

7. **Ghost.** Besides being spooky, these Pokémon are notoriously hard to catch.

8. **Grass.** These Pokémon usually look like animals, but they have vines, leaves, and other plant parts that they use in battle.

9. **Ground.** These sturdy Pokémon like to live close to, even under, the ground.

10. **Ice.** The freezing powers of these Pokémon have a chilling effect on their opponents.

11. **Normal.** They're called Normal because they don't have any powers associated with elements like fire or water. These Pokémon are often the most unusual of all!

12. **Poison.** It's not easy to recover when one of these Pokémon poisons you during an attack.

13. **Psychic.** These Pokémon use spe-

cial mind powers, such as telekinesis, to control the movements and actions of their opponents.

14. **Rock.** They're made of stone, tough as nails, and hard to beat!

15. **Water.** These Pokémon usually live in water, and use water attacks when they battle other Pokémon.

POKé STUFF

Poké Ball. A red-and-white ball that trainers use to capture and hold Pokémon. The Pokémon are released when the trainer throws the ball or pushes a button on the ball.

Pokédex. A handheld computer that trainers carry. It holds information about all of the world's Pokémon.

Meet the Pokémon

In *The Power of One*, some new Pokémon are unveiled, and secrets about the Legendary Pokémon are revealed. Here's a sneak peek at the Pokémon that star in this book.

THE LEGENDARY BIRDS

Articuno: A combination Ice and Flying Pokémon, Articuno has blue feathers and a long, flowing tail. Until now, it has only appeared to doomed people lost in icy mountains. Articuno reigns over Ice Island in the Orange Islands and guards one of three sacred treasures.

Zapdos: A combination Electric and Flying Pokémon, Zapdos has golden yellow feathers and a long orange beak. Zapdos appears from the clouds while blasting huge bolts of lightning. Zapdos reigns over Lightning Island in the Orange Islands and guards one of three sacred treasures.

Moltres: A combination Fire and Flying Pokémon, Moltres has orange-yellow feathers. A fiery crown burns on top of its head, and each flap of its wings creates a stunning display of flames. Moltres reigns over Fire Island in the Orange Islands and protects one of three sacred treasures.

THE NEW POKéMON

Slowking: The evolved form of Slowpoke and Slowbro, Slowking looks like its previous forms but walks on two legs and wears a ruffled collar and majestic silver crown. The Slowking that lives on Shamouti Island can translate Pokémon speech into human speech.

Lugia: Never before seen by human eyes, Lugia is a combination Water and Flying Pokémon that dwells in the depths of the sea. With its sleek white skin and blue belly, Lugia looks like a cross between a seal and an ocean bird. Many trainers believe its power is greater than the three Legendary Bird Pokémon combined.

On an island at the very edge of the Orange Archipelago, a Pokémon stares out at the blue sea.

It is Slowking. The Pokémon has a pink, sturdy body. It wears a majestic silver crown on its head.

A temple set on a circle of smooth stone rises up behind Slowking. Seven pillars ring the circle. The floor of the temple is inscribed with the words of the ancient legend:

Disturb not the harmony of Fire, Ice, or Lightning, lest these titans wreak destruction upon the world in which they

clash. Though the Water's Great Guardian shall arise to quell the fighting, alone its song will fail. Thus the earth shall turn to ash.

Oh Chosen One, into thine hands, bring together all three. Their treasures combined tame the Beast of the Sea.

Slowking knows the words of the legend well. They foretell a time of great destruction.

And now something is stirring. Slowking can feel it.

"Something is wrong," the Pokémon speaks the human words aloud. "It is starting. . . ."

Slowking was not the only one who knew about the legend.

Miles away, in a ship that floated high in the sky, a human tried to figure out the meaning of the words.

Lawrence III.

Tall and handsome, Lawrence III had everything an enterprising man could want. Power. Money. A private museum filled with rare Pokémon.

But Lawrence III was not satisfied. His Pokémon collection was not complete.

Lawrence III sat in a large chair in the center of a circular room.

"'The Beast of the Sea'," he repeated to

himself. "'The Beast of the Sea.' It *must* mean . . ." He recited the words of the legend once again. "'Into thine hands, bring together all three. Their treasures combined tame the Beast of the Sea.'" He focused his steely eyes on a computer screen in front of him.

The computer spoke in a mechanical voice. "Exhaustive scrutiny of the legend reveals that the Titan of Fire is really the Legendary Pokémon Moltres. The Titan of Lightning is Zapdos. And the Titan of Ice is Articuno."

"Moltres, Zapdos, and Articuno," Lawrence III mused. "Any one of them would be a priceless addition to my collection. But if my interpretation is correct, together they are the three keys that unlock the ultimate treasure. Where are they?" he asked the computer.

"I have located Moltres in the vicinity of Shamouti Island," the computer replied.

At its words, a holographic chessboard appeared in the air in front of Lawrence III. Four islands sat in a circle on the grid. One island looked like a volcano. An image of a Flying Pokémon circled it. The Pokémon had yellow feathers. Orange-red flames lit up its wings and head.

"Then let's get started," Lawrence III said coolly.

The arms of the chair were lined with buttons and switches. Stelthius pressed one of the buttons, and the floating ship lurched forward and sailed over the sea.

At the same time, an image of the ship appeared on the holographic chessboard.

The ship was constructed of silver, donut-shaped chambers stacked one on top of the other. Antennas, metal arms, and other equipment jutted out.

Soon they reached Moltres's island — Fire Island.

The Pokémon was nowhere to be found. But Lawrence III spotted a cave carved into the volcano.

Lawrence III orchestrated the capture from his chair. With another touch of a button, ice bombs exploded out of the ship and bombarded the cave. The round bombs looked like giant snowballs. They froze everything they touched and sent frigid blasts of air inside the cave.

The flaming Pokémon flew out of the cave, confused and hurt.

Boom! Lawrence III hurled more ice bombs at the legendary bird.

The freezing bombs stung Moltres. It cried out in pain.

Then Lawrence III sent out traps to capture the weakened bird. The traps looked like metal hoops, and they moved in the air as though they had minds of their own. An electric force field crackled inside each hoop. The hoops relentlessly pursued the Legendary Pokémon.

Moltres struggled. Lawrence III hit it with more ice bombs.

Moltres could resist no longer. The metal hoops surrounded Moltres, forming a ball-shaped cage.

The cage flew back to the floating ship, and a door opened.

Lawrence III managed a small, greedy smile as he watched his triumph on the chessboard.

"Yet another addition to my collection. Moltres, once thought to be the Titan of Fire," Lawrence III said. "It's like a simple game of chess. Next I'll capture Zapdos and Articuno."

Lawrence III stood up. He gazed out the window at the open sea.

"And if I'm right, capturing these three Pokémon, will flush out the jewel of my collection," Lawrence III said. "A Pokémon never before seen by human eyes."

Lawrence III's eyes gleamed. "Lugia, you will be mine!"

Chapter One

A Sudden Storm

"**W**hat a great day!" Ash Ketchum said, looking at the clear sky above. Below him, blue-green ocean waves lapped against the speedboat.

Ash's friend Misty agreed. "It's really wonderful, isn't it?" On most days, Misty was in a bad mood — usually about something Ash said or did. But today her blue eyes sparkled happily. A light breeze played with her orange ponytail.

"*Togi, togi!*" Misty's tiny Pokémon, Togepi, flapped its little arms and legs happily.

Ash's Pokémon, Pikachu, stood on the railing of the boat. His friend Tracey Sketchit sat on the deck, drawing the scene in a notepad.

1

Ash and Misty had first traveled to the Orange Islands weeks ago, on an errand for Ash's friend and mentor, Professor Oak. When their errand was complete, Ash had decided to explore the islands.

As a Pokémon trainer, Ash's goal in life was to become a Pokémon Master, someone who had captured and trained many different types of Pokémon and had earned membership in the Pokémon League. To become a Master, he'd need lots of experience, and he knew he'd get it in the Orange Islands. So far, he had seen new Pokémon and participated in Pokémon battles unlike any he'd ever been in before. He didn't know what new challenge awaited him next.

"We lucked out when we met Maren," Ash told Misty.

"You're right," Misty said. "This boat is super fast."

On the top deck, a woman with dark green hair steered the boat. She wore a red nylon jacket and pants. Maren smiled down at Ash and Misty.

"I'm always happy to help out Pokémon trainers," she said.

Tracey Sketchit joined his friends at the

stern of the boat. The dark-haired boy wore shorts and a T-shirt.

"Why don't we let our Pokémon get some sun while we've got the chance?" he suggested.

"Why not?" Maren said. "We have plenty of time before we reach the next island. Relax a little."

Ash threw three Poké Balls in the air. "Come on out, everyone!"

The Poké Balls burst open in an explosion of light, and three Pokémon appeared.

Squirtle, a Water Pokémon that looked like a cute turtle, hugged Ash.

Bulbasaur smiled and walked over to Squirtle. A Grass Pokémon, Bulbasaur looked like a blue-green dinosaur with a plant bulb on its back.

Lapras, a blue Water Pokémon that looked like a friendly sea monster, splashed into the waves next to the boat.

Two more Pokémon landed in the water. Misty let out Goldeen, a frilly orange goldfish Pokémon, and Staryu, which looked like a large starfish.

On deck, Misty's orange Psyduck waddled around, holding its head.

Tracey's Pokémon, Marill and Venonat, watched Psyduck and giggled. Scyther, another of Tracey's Pokémon, practiced its battle moves alongside them.

Ash decided to let out Charizard, a hot-tempered Fire and Flying Pokémon that looked like a lizard with wings. As soon as it was out, Charizard breathed a hot jet of fire into the air.

Ash held out a Poké Ball and quickly recalled Charizard. He threw out another ball, and a big, round Pokémon that looked like a bear appeared. Snorlax plopped down on the deck, but it was so heavy that the boat started to sink. Ash quickly recalled Snorlax, too.

"At least my other Pokémon are having fun," Ash remarked. Ash decided to relax for a little bit. He was wearing his usual outfit: a red-and-white cap over his messy dark hair, jeans, and a vest over a short-sleeved shirt. The sun felt nice and warm on his bare arms.

While Ash basked in the sun, the Pokémon played happily together on the deck of the boat.

All but one.

Pikachu, Ash's yellow Electric Pokémon, stood at the helm of the boat. Pikachu studied the sky, worried. It frowned.

Suddenly, thick black clouds began to cover the sky. Within moments, it was as dark as night.

A strong wind whipped around the boat. The once calm waves began to churn, rocking the boat back and forth. Hard rain pelted the deck.

"It's a storm!" Maren cried. "Everyone take cover!"

Ash reached for his Poké Balls. It should have been easy to recall his Pokémon, but the wind was blowing hard — too hard. With every ounce of strength he had, he held up the Poké Balls. Squirtle, Bulbasaur, and Lapras disappeared in a flash of red light.

Misty and Tracey struggled to get their Pokémon safely back into their Poké Balls as well. When they were done, Misty hugged Togepi tightly and hunched down on the deck.

Ash sighed with relief. The Pokémon were safe.

Then he remembered.

"Pikachu!" Ash cried.

Ash fought against the wind. He made it to the helm of the boat, where Pikachu clutched the rail. The wind was about to carry away the yellow lightning mouse.

"I've got you, Pikachu!" Ash cried. He grabbed Pikachu tightly and didn't let go.

A giant wave rocked the boat. Rain lashed at Ash's face.

A bolt of lightning lit up the dark sky, and in the flash, Ash could see that they had sailed near an island.

Another wave hit the boat, carrying them closer to the rocky shore.

"Hold on, everyone!" Maren shouted. "We're out of control!"

Chapter Two

Enemies and Friends

Ash and his friends weren't the only ones surprised by the sudden storm.

Just below the surface of the ocean, two people and a Pokémon paddled a submarine that looked like a giant orange Magikarp.

They were Jessie, James, and Meowth, a trio of Pokémon thieves known as Team Rocket. They were always looking for Pokémon to steal, and Ash's Pikachu was the one they wanted most of all. They were following Ash and Pikachu all over the Orange Islands and were pretty close to catching up to them when the storm started.

Jessie, a tall teenage girl with long red

hair, looked through a periscope. A school of real Magikarp swam past the scope.

"Those Magikarp sure are in a hurry to get somewhere," Jessie remarked.

"Meowth!" said the scratch cat Pokémon. "That sure sounds *fishy* to me!"

"Why are we wasting time talking about Magikarp?" asked James, a teenage boy with blue hair. "We're here to grab that precious Pikachu."

Suddenly, an underwater current locked on the submarine. The vessel was hurled to the surface of the sea.

"Uh, do we have carp insurance?" Jessie asked.

Jessie peered through the periscope. Jagged black rocks surrounded them at every turn.

A surface wave crashed against the submarine. The wave tossed them against a sharp rock, and the Magikarp sub cracked open like a nut.

"What's happening, Jess?" James asked.

"It's the same as always," Jessie said. "It looks like we're about to be . . ."

"Filet of fish!" finished Meowth, as Team Rocket was hurtled through the air by another wave.

Miles away, the sudden clouds and rain startled Ash Ketchum's mother. She was working in her garden with the help of Mr. Mime, her Psychic Pokémon.

Ash's mentor, Professor Oak, rode up on his bicycle. Professor Oak had given Ash his first Pokémon — Pikachu — and started Ash on his Pokémon journey. Since then, he and Ash's mother had become good friends.

Mr. Mime fetched an umbrella as the first drops started. It held the umbrella over Ash's mother.

"This storm is certainly unexpected, isn't it?" Oak asked.

Mrs. Ketchum nodded. Then her eyes widened in surprise.

Instead of rain, white flakes fell from the sky.

"Snow?" she exclaimed. "But it's summer!"

The snow ended as suddenly as it started.

The sky glowed a soft pink. A flock of Pidgey flew overhead.

"Mime! Mime!" Mr. Mime said worriedly.

Then the ground beneath them began to rumble. A herd of Diglett, Pokémon that looked like big earthworms, tore up the ground under Professor Oak's feet. They were headed in the same direction as the Pidgey.

"What's happening?" Mrs. Ketchum asked. "I've never seen Mimey so upset."

Professor Oak looked thoughtful. "This is very serious. There must be some kind of global disturbance in the weather. Someone or something has upset the balance of nature. Pokémon are much more sensitive to these things than humans."

Ash's mother looked worried. "What can we do?"

Professor Oak hopped on his bike. "I'll contact Professor Ivy in the Orange Islands," he said. "We must get to the bottom of this!"

Chapter Three

Shamouti Island

Ash closed his eyes, hugged Pikachu, and braced for the worst.

There was a thud, and the boat lurched. Then there was calm.

Ash opened his eyes. They had landed safely on the beach. A stone wall bordered the far end of the beach. Steps led up to a small village.

"Pikachu, we're all right!" Ash said, smiling.

But Pikachu didn't return the smile. Its eyes were clouded with worry.

Misty's voice came from the other end of the boat. "Oh, my gosh!" she said. "What's that?"

A procession of strange birdlike crea-tures were lined up on the stone wall. The creatures had human bodies and large bird heads with brightly colored feathers. They carried strange-looking drums and rattles.

"Caw! Caw! Caw!" The bird creatures cried loudly and jumped off the wall and onto the sand.

Tracey scrambled to hide behind Ash and Misty.

Ash froze. What strange thing were they up against now?

Then one of the creatures spoke.

"Hey, Maren!"

The creature took off its head to reveal the face of a pretty teenage girl with brown hair. Ash felt foolish. They were just people wearing masks!

Maren climbed down to the shore.

"Carol," she said, holding out her hand, "I haven't seen you in years!"

Carol hugged her. "The last time I saw you, we were in school on Mandarin Island."

"Why are you wearing that costume?" Maren asked her friend.

"We're having a festival," Carol replied.

Maren nodded. "Are you still playing the role of the festival maiden? Where's your flute?"

"I'm too old for that," said Carol. "My little sister's taken over the role. Where is she, anyway?"

A voice answered Carol. "Who are you calling little?"

Ash looked up. A girl his age stood on a rock by the steps. She wasn't dressed in costume, though. A cap sat on top of her long brown hair. She wore dark sunglasses, a tank top, and jeans.

"I'm no festival maiden!" the girl said, scowling. "You'd think after a few centuries you'd all have outgrown this dorky festival."

Carol sighed. "That's my little sister, Melody. She's supposed to be the festival maiden — whether she likes it or not."

"Times are changing," Maren said.

Ash cleared his throat loudly. He hated to be left out of anything.

"Oh, I'm sorry," Maren said. "These are my friends, Misty, Tracey, and Ash. Ash is competing in the Orange League. He's a Pokémon trainer."

The costumed villagers all gasped. Then they yelled and cheered, banging on their instruments.

A man wearing a blue bird mask with big red eyes stepped up to Ash. He took off the mask. Underneath, he had a weathered face and a white mustache.

"If you are truly a Pokémon trainer," the man said, "then *you* are the Chosen One!"

Chapter Four

The Chosen One?

"What are you talking about?" Ash asked.

"The ancient legend tells of your arrival," the man said. "Only with your help can the Water's Great Guardian vanquish the great titans of Fire, Ice, and Lightning. In your hands, Oh Chosen One, rests the world and its fate."

"It *does*?" Ash asked.

The old man smiled. "Don't let it go to your head," he said. "I say this every year. It's all part of the festival tradition."

He put the mask back on.

"That's my father, Tobias," Carol told Ash. "He's a little dramatic sometimes. But he's right about one thing — we do need a Pokémon trainer to act in our festival. It's tradition."

Melody approached Ash. She lowered her sunglasses. "I guess you'll do. Here's the traditional welcome." She planted a kiss on Ash's cheek.

Ash blushed. Behind him, Misty scowled.

"We might as well go to the festival and have a good time," Maren said.

Misty's sour expression changed to a smile. "Sounds good to me," she said. "I'm hungry!"

"And I'd love to sketch your traditional costumes," Tracey said. "They're fascinating. They remind me of ancient drawings I've seen of the Legendary Pokémon."

Ash picked up Pikachu and hoisted the Pokémon on top of his shoulders. "Let's go, then!"

The villagers cheered happily and started up the stone steps. Ash and the others followed.

More villagers were lined up on each side of the street. Other people in costume were marching in a parade. A group of puppeteers carried a long blue Gyarados puppet on a stick. The puppet, which looked like a sea monster, seemed to dance on ocean waves.

Ash got caught up in the spectacle. Musicians banged drums and shook rattles. Little kids ran around, wearing fake bird beaks.

The parade ended up in front of a large open hut. Long tables were set up with tropical fruit and other delicious food. Torches lit up the darkness.

Carol took off her mask. "Now we feast!" she shouted.

Ash found a table with Misty and Tracey. They happily stuffed themselves with food. Togepi snacked on fruit. But Pikachu barely picked at the food. It didn't have much of an appetite.

Normally, Ash would have noticed that something was wrong with Pikachu. But the festival was too exciting.

"I wonder where Melody is," Ash said. He wouldn't admit it to his friends, but he thought she was an interesting girl. He'd never met anyone quite like her.

Suddenly, the lilting notes of a flute floated through the night air. The crowd hushed.

A girl in a flowing white dress stepped into the hut. She wore a crown and a necklace of red flowers. She played a flute made out of a white conch shell.

"I think that's Melody now," Tracey said.

"Melody?" Ash asked. "That doesn't look anything like her!"

The girl finished the song on the flute. Then she walked toward Ash's table.

Now Ash could tell. It *was* Melody.

Melody held up her arms and spoke in a theatrical voice.

"Hear ye all! From the trio of islands ancient spheres you shall take. For between life and death, the difference you'll make," Melody chanted. Then she faced Ash. "Oh, Chosen One! Climb to the shrine and right what is wrong and the world will be healed by the Guardian's song."

"What are you talking about?" Ash asked. "What am I supposed to do?"

"Oh it won't be very hard, Ash," Melody said, sounding like her old self. "Listen, don't take this too seriously. I have to say this every year. It's part of the script."

"Melody!" Carol scolded from across the room. "Please stick to the tradition, okay?"

"Okay," Melody said with a little sigh. She turned back to Ash. "Here's what you're supposed to do. You must collect three glass treasures from the three islands just offshore and place them in the temple on this island. Then I celebrate by playing a song, and that's it!"

Ash was confused. "Treasures? Where are they?"

Melody took three pieces of fruit out of a bowl. One by one, she placed them in Ash's hands.

"You'll find one treasure on Fire Island, one on Ice Island, and one on Lightning Island," she said. "Don't worry. You can reach all the islands by boat, and there are stairs leading up to the temples. It's pretty easy."

The Chosen One. Three treasures. Ash was not one to refuse a challenge. He stood up, a look of determination on his face.

"I'll go right now!" Ash said.

"There's no need to hurry," Melody said.

"The festival lasts all day tomorrow. You can do it in the morning."

But Ash was eager, as always. "Never delay a good deed. That's my motto!"

Misty rolled her eyes. "That's just like Ash. He has to make a big deal out of everything."

Maren overheard them. She walked to their table. "Never delay a good deed. I like that! I'll get the boat."

"Thanks," Ash said. "Are you coming, Misty?"

Misty frowned. "You're the Chosen One, not me. If you want to go on a wild goose chase in the middle of the night, then you're on your own."

"Fine," Ash said. "Pikachu, let's go!"

On the other side of Shamouti Island, Slowking guarded the ancient temple. The Pokémon stared worriedly at the churning sea.

More rain started to fall from the clouds. Bursts of angry lightning exploded in the sky.

"'Disturb not the harmony of Fire, Ice,

or Lightning, lest these titans wreak destruction upon the world in which they clash,'" Slowking said, repeating the old legend. "Generations of Slowking safeguard the legend with no problems. I'm on the job two weeks and someone has set the wheels in motion." Slowking paused. "There has been a shift in the balance of power. The legend is coming to pass."

Chapter Five

The Quest Begins

Ash and Pikachu stood next to Maren as she piloted the speedboat.

During the festival, the storm had quieted down, but now it was springing up again. The rocky motion of the boat made Ash feel queasy. And the cold rain seemed to penetrate his skin.

"I thought Melody said fetching the treasures would be easy," Ash said. "This seems pretty hard to me!"

Maren pointed to an island topped by a big volcano. "Don't worry, Ash," she said. "We're almost at Fire Island. I'll get us there safely."

Maren steered the boat toward the island, struggling all the way. Rain, wind, and waves made the journey almost impossible.

Then suddenly, there was quiet. The rain and wind stopped.

"It's cleared up!" Ash said.

"But why haven't the seas calmed?" Maren asked, concerned.

Ash looked down at the swirling water. Maren was right. Strong currents pulled the boat back and forth.

Maren set her mouth in a straight line and stared straight ahead.

They were almost at the island now. But tall, jagged rocks blocked their path.

Maren expertly steered the ship through the rocks.

"I feel like a mouse Pokémon in a maze!" Ash remarked.

Pikachu didn't even smile at the joke.

Crack! A hideous sound caused Ash to jump. The boat stalled.

"The rudder's broken!" Maren said. "I can't steer without it!"

Then the boat lurched forward and slammed onto the rocky shore.

A look of relief crossed Maren's face, but she was pale and shaken. "We made it," she said. "But we'd better stay put for a while. This weather is too unpredictable to —"

"*Pika!*" Pikachu jumped off the boat and ran up a set of stone steps.

Melody had said there were stairs leading up to the temples. Pikachu was going to find the treasure!

"Stay with the boat," Ash told Maren. "I've got to go after Pikachu!"

Back on Shamouti Island, Melody, Carol, Misty, and Tracey looked out anxiously at the rough waters.

"It's too dangerous out there," Melody said. She turned to her sister. "Lend me a boat, Carol."

"What do you plan to do in a storm like this?" Carol asked.

"Right now Ash and Maren are in danger because of our silly tradition," Melody said. "I'm the one who asked Ash to be in our festival. I just hope they're all right."

Melody spun around and walked down to the dock. Misty and Tracey followed.

"What are you doing here?" Melody asked as she readied the boat.

"Ash is my friend," Misty said. "I'm going to help."

"Me, too," agreed Tracey.

Melody smiled.

"From the look of things, Ash is going to need all the help he can get," Melody said. "Let's board."

Melody, Misty, and Tracey climbed into the boat. It was smaller than Maren's boat, but it was sleek and powerful all the same.

As Melody started the engines, three soaking wet figures stealthily climbed on board. They hid under a black tarp.

It was Team Rocket, of course.

"When we blasted out of our submarine, I thought all was lost," James said.

"But now we're right where we want to be," Jessie said. "Ash's phony friends will take us right to him . . ."

". . . and Pikachu will finally be ours!" finished Meowth.

Chapter Six

Lawrence III's Next Move

Back in Pallet Town, Ash's mom and Professor Oak sat anxiously in front of a TV. A reporter wearing a rain hat and slicker spoke. Behind him, a storm raged.

"Experts believe that the weather disasters occuring in all parts of the globe are due to a powerful phenomenon deep beneath the surface of the ocean," said the reporter. "This 'underwater river' has snaked its way around the planet. It is disrupting ocean currents, weather patterns, and the entire global climate. Officials have nicknamed the 'underwater river' the beast of the sea, because of its great destructive powers.

"The problem with the current seems to

be located in the Orange Islands," he continued. "Pokémon all over the world are traveling there. Experts believe the Pokémon sense danger."

"But that's where Ash and his friends are right now!" Ash's mom cried out in fear.

Meanwhile, high up in the floating ship, Lawrence III sat in his chair, watching a holographic image of the Orange Islands on his chessboard. He did not pay attention to the storm raging outside. He was focused on his goal: to capture the next Legendary Pokémon.

Lawrence III studied Fire Island. He had captured Moltres, leaving that island empty.

Two islands away, Lightning Island waited for him. An image of a Flying Pokémon appeared around the island. This Pokémon had bright golden feathers that jutted out of its body like lightning bolts.

"Zapdos, the Pokémon known in legend as the Titan of Lightning," Lawrence III said. "Soon I will add Zapdos to my collection."

Lawrence III pressed a button, and the ship sailed toward Lightning Island.

Chapter Seven

Zapdos, Titan of Lightning

Back on Fire Island, Ash followed Pikachu up the stairs.

At the top of the steps sat a crude hut made of slabs of stone. Pikachu disappeared inside.

"Hold up, Pikachu!" Ash called out.

Ash entered the temple. Puffing and panting, he tried to focus his eyes in the dark. Where was the treasure? What was he looking for?

On the far wall of the temple rested a statue of a birdlike Pokémon. The Pokémon's mouth was open wide.

Pikachu hopped up on the statue.

"Pika! Pika!" Pikachu said urgently.

Ash looked closely at the statue. Inside the bird's mouth was a small round globe about the size of an orange.

An orange . . . then Ash remembered. Melody had put three pieces of fruit in his hands. This must be the treasure!

Ash reached into the stone bird's mouth and grabbed the orb. He pulled and pulled, but the treasure wouldn't budge.

Then suddenly, the orb began to glow with a soft red light.

"Whoa," Ash said.

The treasure slipped out of its hold and into Ash's hands.

"I've got it!" Ash cried. "Thanks, Pikachu!"

"Pika," said the Pokémon, nodding. Then Pikachu darted out of the temple.

"Why are you in such a hurry, Pikachu?" Ash muttered. But he took off after his friend.

Pikachu started to race back down the stairs. Above them, the sky grew even darker.

Then a voice stopped Ash and Pikachu in their tracks.

"We've got you right where we want you!"

Ash and Pikachu spun around. Meowth, Jessie, and James stood on a rock overhanging the steps. They looked pretty pleased with themselves.

"Prepare for more trouble than you've ever seen!" Jessie said.

"Make it double. We're on the big screen!" said James.

Ash couldn't believe it.

"Could you guys cut your motto short this time?" he asked. "The weather's looking pretty rough."

"Too bad. We're going to take Pikachu, whether you like it or not!" Jessie threatened.

Ash tensed, ready for a battle.

Then a humming sound filled the air.

Team Rocket looked puzzled, and then they looked up.

A small boat rigged with billowing sails flew up the rock.

It was Melody, Misty, and Tracey!

The boat crash-landed on Team Rocket, halting their attack.

Melody jumped out of the boat.

"Ash, you had us so worried!" she

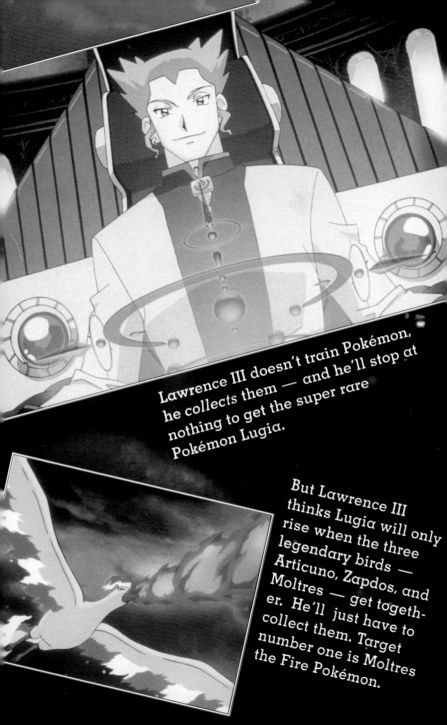

Lawrence III doesn't train Pokémon, he collects them — and he'll stop at nothing to get the super rare Pokémon Lugia.

But Lawrence III thinks Lugia will only rise when the three legendary birds — Articuno, Zapdos, and Moltres — get together. He'll just have to collect them. Target number one is Moltres the Fire Pokémon.

Oh no! The biggest storm ever seen erupts. The world's Pokémon sense danger and head for the Orange Islands.

Team Rocket is Orange Islands bound, too. Their submarine gets caught up in a frantic school of Magikarp.

Professor Oak and Ash Ketchum's mom are worried. Ash and his friends are training their Pokémon in the Orange Islands.

Ash, Misty, and Tracey crash the annual Legend Festival on Shamouti Island.

Treasure hunt time! Melody tells Ash that at
every festival someone is picked to collect three
treasures from the islands of Ice, Lightning, and
Fire. This year Ash is the Chosen One!

Ash and Pikachu are
determined to find the
treasures.

They find the first two
treasures on the islands of
Fire and Ice.

With Moltres gone, Zapdos is ready to take over Fire Island. Pikachu tries to stop Zapdos. Instead they all get sucked up into Lawrence III's ship.

Lawrence III keeps his Pokémon collection in super strong cages. That is so wrong! Ash, Misty, Tracey, Melody, and even Team Rocket use their Pokémon to free Moltres.

Lawrence III's ship crashes on Lightning Island.

Zapdos, Moltres, and Articuno break free — but now they're angry! They battle one another for control.

Uh-oh! Melody realizes Ash really *is* the Chosen One! Slowking tells them the rest of the story. Lugia will rise from the sea to save the world — but it won't work until Ash finds the third treasure.

The legendary Lugia rises from the
depths of the ocean to help Ash.
Can it save the world?

If Ash places three treasures on the Shamouti Island altar, Lugia's song will stop the storm and soothe the savage birds. Lugia will protect Ash. But who will protect Lugia from Lawrence III's evil clutches?

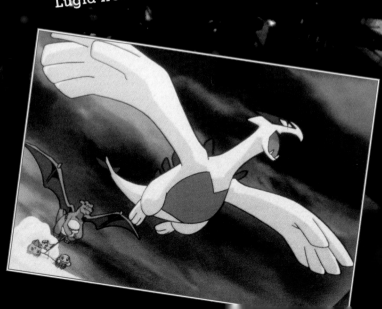

If the world is destroyed, there won't be any Pokémon to steal. Team Rocket decides to "protect the world from devastation." Jessie, James, and Meowth prepare to fight – on Ash's side!

Hang on, Ash and Pikachu! Lugia flies them back toward the altar with the third treasure.

Pokémon from all over the world gather
at the Orange Islands to watch and wait.
Did Ash do it?

Ash's courage pulls him through! Ash and Pikachu place the third treasure on the altar. Melody plays Lugia's song on her flute, and the legendary birds' fiery tempers are chilled. The storm is over. The world is saved!

Saving the world is tough work — even for a future Pokémon Master and his Pikachu! *Pika, pika, chu!*

scolded. "You should have just stayed back at the party like I said. We all wouldn't be stuck out here on this island if you had just listened to me in the first place."

Misty joined her. "I told you Ash was stubborn," she said.

"Hey! Get off my back," Ash said. "I got the treasure, just like I said I would." He held up the glowing orb.

At the word "treasure," Team Rocket crawled out from under the boat.

"Did you say treasure?" Jessie asked, her eyes gleaming greedily.

"Don't even think about it," Ash said. "You're not getting Pikachu. And you're *not* getting this treasure!" He stowed the globe safely in his vest pocket.

"We'll see about that," James said, trying to stand up.

"Zaaaaaw! Zaaaaaaaw!"

"What now?" Ash asked.

Golden lightning bolts flashed in the dark sky. A huge Flying Pokémon swooped down through the lightning.

"Zapdos!" Ash said, amazed.

The Legendary Pokémon had shining

gold feathers and a long orange beak. It seemed to glow with electric energy.

Zap! Zap! Zapdos hurled more golden lightning bolts down at the island.

The bolts hit two large rocks, splitting them in half.

"Why is it attacking us?" Tracey wondered.

"I don't know," Ash said. "But we've got to find cover."

"How are we supposed to hide from lightning bolts that can split rocks?" Melody asked.

Zapdos swooped down toward the temple. Pikachu sprang into action. The small Electric Pokémon jumped onto the front of Melody's boat. Sparks sizzled on its cheeks as it built up an electric charge.

"Don't do it, Pikachu!" Ash pleaded. Pikachu was powerful but not powerful enough to take down Zapdos.

Pikachu didn't waver.

"Pikaaaaaaaaaa!" it cried, aiming a huge electric blast at Zapdos.

The energy hit Zapdos with full force, but it didn't phase the Legendary Pokémon.

Zapdos absorbed the attack without flinching.

Then it aimed a lightning bolt at Pikachu. The bolt zapped Pikachu, knocking it off the boat.

"Pikachu!" Ash cried.

Zapdos flew down and sat on top of the stone temple. It folded its wings. Its body shimmered with blue electric energy. The blue glow covered the island like a blanket.

Pikachu ran up to the temple, angry at the large Pokémon.

"Pikachuuuuuu!" Pikachu aimed three bolts of electricity, one after the other, at Zapdos.

Once again, Zapdos absorbed the blasts.

"Zaaaaaw! Zaaaaaw! Zaaaaaw!" Zapdos cried out.

"Pikachu's pretty tough," Jessie said. "But Zapdos isn't even feeling those attacks."

"Those aren't attacks," Meowth said. "Pikachu's trying to talk to Zapdos!"

Ash knew Meowth could translate the language of other Pokémon.

"What is it saying?" he asked Meowth.

"It's saying, 'What are you doing over

here on Fire Island, Zapdos? And where's Moltres?'" Meowth translated.

"Good question," Jessie remarked.

"Zaaaaaw! Zaaaaaw! Zaaaaaw!" Zapdos cried again.

"Now Zapdos is answering," Meowth said. "Zapdos says, 'Moltres used to rule here. But now that Moltres is gone, Lightning shall rule over Fire. I claim this island as my own.'"

"I guess Moltres flew the coop!" James said.

Angry again, Zapdos focused its attention on Pikachu. It aimed a golden lightning bolt at the small Electric Pokémon.

Pikachu retaliated with a powerful Thunderbolt. The two blasts met in midair, causing a blue electric current to flow between Zapdos and Pikachu.

"Pikachuuuu!" Pikachu tried with all its might to break the current. *Bam!* The force of the effort threw Pikachu back several feet.

The electric currents swirled in the air like blue whips. Ash and the others scrambled to dodge the dangerous energy.

Then suddenly, the electric whips began

to flow straight up to the sky. Zapdos let out a cry of alarm.

The Pokémon's electricity flowed up into the clouds.

"Something is sucking up Zapdos's electricity!" Tracey said.

Chapter Eight

Captured!

At Tracey's words, a giant craft appeared from behind the clouds. Ash couldn't believe his eyes. It looked like some kind of floating spaceship. The ship was stealing the blue electric current from Zapdos.

Zapdos looked weakened but not defeated. It flew off its perch on the temple, breaking the link with the strange ship.

Metal doors on the bottom of the ship opened. A metal, diamond-shaped hoop flew out and zoomed toward Zapdos.

Three more hoops shot out and joined the first. They circled Zapdos. The Flying Pokémon fought them off with one explosion of electricity after another.

"Everyone get in the boat!" Melody shouted. "Maybe we can get out of here while it's distracted."

Ash, Pikachu, Misty, and Tracey ran to Melody's boat. Even Team Rocket jumped on board.

Zapdos dove to the ground, trying to escape the hoops. The hoops dove after it, as if they were locked on target.

"Zaaaaaw!" Zapdos screamed as two of the hoops surrounded it, forming a kind of trap. The Flying Pokémon frantically flapped its wings. The hoops held fast.

The other two hoops locked on Melody's boat. Ash watched in amazement as the hoops formed a trap around the boat, just like the one around Zapdos.

Then the hoops rose into the air and carried Zapdos and the boat up into the sky.

"We've been captured!" Ash yelled.

"We sure have," said Misty. "But by what?"

The boat floated up through the metal doors of the ship. The doors closed underneath them with a mechanical whir. Then they traveled up through a tall metal tunnel. Two more doors opened, and they entered a large, circular room.

The trapped Zapdos was already there. The bird rattled its metal cage fiercely, but it could not get out.

Then Ash noticed that Zapdos was not the only Pokémon locked up there. Next to it, in a similar cage, was a yellow Pokémon with flaming wings.

"Moltres!" Tracey exclaimed. "Another Legendary Pokémon."

"*Meowth!* This must be why Moltres was missing from Fire Island," Meowth said. "Somebody dragged it up here."

"Who?" Ash asked. "Who's behind all this?"

The floor opened in the center of the room, and a platform rose out of the opening. On top of the platform, a tall man sat in a chair. Buttons and switches lined the arms of the strange chair.

The man stood up and walked toward Ash and the others.

"My deepest apologies," he said. "I am Lawrence III. I only intended to capture Zapdos. I did not mean to capture you as well."

He gestured to the two captured Pokémon. "You are my first human guests here,"
he said. "What do you think? Moltres, Bird
of Fire. Zapdos, Bird of Lightning. The
newest additions to my collection. Of
course, without Articuno it's not a complete
set, but . . ."

"That's disgusting! The way you talk its
like Pokémon are just things to *collect* like
dolls or stamps!" Misty shouted. "What kind
of trainer are you?"

"I'm not a Pokémon trainer," Lawrence
III responded coldly. "I'm a *collector*. I began
my collection with a Mew card, and now I
have all this. Legendary Pokémon have always been my passion. And soon my collection will be legendary!"

Lawrence III returned to his chair. He
pressed a button, and a holographic chessboard appeared. Ash recognized images of
the islands surrounding Shamouti Island.

An image of a Flying Pokémon flew
around Ice Island.

"Uh, would you mind getting us back
to Shamouti Island?" Ash asked him. "I
was right in the middle of something important."

"I would love to let you go," Lawrence III said. "But there is no time to waste. I must capture the third Legendary Bird Pokémon first: Articuno, known in legend as the Titan of Ice."

"The legend?" Melody said to herself. "Could it be . . ."

Lawrence III pressed a button on his chair, and the force field around Melody's boat vanished.

"Feel free to walk around and enjoy my collection," he said. Then he pressed another button, and his chair sank back down into the floor.

Ash jumped out of the boat.

"We've got to find a way out of this place," Ash said.

Melody nodded. "You're right. That guy mentioned something about Articuno being part of the legend. If he's right, then the world's in big trouble."

"What are you talking about?" Ash asked.

"The legend says, 'Disturb not the harmony of Fire, Ice, or Lightning, lest these titans wreck destruction upon the world,'" Melody said. "If Articuno is the Titan of Ice, then Moltres and Zapdos must be the Titans of Fire and Lightning."

"That makes sense!" Ash said. "But the legend says not to disturb them. These guys look pretty disturbed to me." He pointed to Moltres and Zapdos.

Melody nodded solemnly. "Exactly," she said. "The balance of power between Ice, Fire, and Lightning is all off. The legend is coming true. And that means . . ."

The horrible truth dawned on Ash.

"That means the world is going to end!" Ash cried.

Chapter Nine

Newsbreak!

While Ash was trying to escape from Lawrence III's ship, Professor Oak prepared for a news conference on a nearby island.

Professor Oak had traveled to the lab of his friend Professor Ivy on Valencia Island in the Orange Archipelago. Together, they thought they could find out what was going wrong.

Ash's mother had come along, too. "My son is out there somewhere," Mrs. Ketchum had said. "I have to know that he's safe."

A reporter in a dark suit began the newscast.

"As we've reported, we believe that the

dangerous weather is being caused by a change in the underwater sea current," the reporter said. "Now we know that the trouble in the current is happening near Shamouti Island, here in the Orange Islands."

An image appeared on a TV monitor. The film showed hundreds, maybe thousands of Pokémon swimming, flying, and walking toward Shamouti Island.

"The Pokémon of the world are moving toward Shamouti Island," the reporter continued. "Water Pokémon are coming by sea, while Pokémon unable to make the crossing are gathering at points of land nearest to Shamouti Island."

The reporter turned to Professor Oak and Professor Ivy, who were seated at a table in Professor Ivy's lab.

"We will now hear opinions on this phenomenon from two eminent scientists and Pokémon experts," he said. "Professor Oak, what is causing the change in the undersea current?"

"Near Shamouti lie the islands of Fire, Ice, and Lightning, home to the legendary birds Moltres, Articuno, and Zapdos," Professor Oak explained. "I fear that these birds are somehow involved."

"How so, professor?" the reporter asked.

"It's possible that someone has disrupted the harmony between Zapdos, Articuno, and Moltres," Professor Oak answered. "That would cause an imbalance of power between Lightning, Ice, and Fire. This imbalance would be enough to form a powerful underwater current — this churning beast of the sea we are experiencing."

"And why would an imbalance of power in the Orange Islands cause a storm in the entire world?" the reporter inquired.

"Ancient writings from many different cultures say that this area is the source of all the waters of the world," Professor Oak replied. "Scientists have argued against this idea throughout history. But it makes sense in a way — especially if you think about what forms when fire and ice are combined. If a beastly underwater current began in this area, it could ultimately flood the entire planet!"

Professor Oak looked thoughtful. "I don't believe the worst has happened —

yet," he said. "The balance must be restored if we want to avert disaster."

"Thank you, Professor Oak," the reporter said. He turned to Professor Ivy. "Can you tell us why the Pokémon are coming to Shamouti Island?"

Professor Ivy looked calm and professional. "The Pokémon are trying to save the planet from destruction," she said. "They may not be able to do anything, but because they are acutely in tune with the balance of nature, the urge to correct this imbalance is causing them to gather."

"We are going to travel to Shamouti Island by helicopter to see what else we can learn," Professor Oak added.

"Thank you," the reporter said. He looked into the camera. "We've heard from the experts. Will this balance be restored? Will disaster be avoided?"

The reporter paused dramatically.

"There is nothing to do but watch and wait . . . and hope for a miracle!"

Chapter Ten

Midair Explosion

Back on Lawrence III's floating ship, Ash and the others tried to figure out what to do.

"Pikachu, you must have known something was wrong all along," Ash told his Pokémon. "That's why you were acting so worried."

"*Pika,*" Pikachu nodded.

"Well, we've got to do something," Ash said.

Team Rocket joined Ash and his friends.

"We'll help you!" Jessie said.

"I thought you'd *like* to see the world destroyed," Ash said. "You're bad guys, aren't you?"

"But if the world is destroyed, there won't be any more Pokémon to steal!" James whined.

"We'll be out of work!" Jessie wailed.

Team Rocket held one another and sobbed.

"We have to help Moltres and Zapdos first," Misty said. "We've got to free them!"

"Right!" Ash said. He ran against the cage that held Moltres, crashing into the metal bars. He didn't even make a dent.

Pikachu aimed bursts of sizzling electricity at the metal bars. The bars hummed a little, but that was about it.

"We need more power!" Ash yelled. "Charizard, I choose you!"

The big Lizard Pokémon exploded from a Poké Ball. Without waiting for Ash's command, it blasted the metal cage with fire.

The bars glowed with orange heat, but they held fast.

"I can't believe it," Misty said. "Electricity won't work. Fire won't work. What are these bars made of, anyway?"

"I bet there's a force field protecting the cage," Tracey said. "It must be very strong."

Jessie wiped a tear from her eye. "Then I guess *we'll* have to give it a try. James, Weezing!"

"Coming right up," James said. He threw out a Poké Ball, and a Poison Pokémon with two heads burst out. Weezing looked like a cloud of purple sludge.

James pointed to the cage that held Zapdos.

"Weezing, break that force field!"

"Weezing!" the Pokémon bellowed in a deep voice.

Weezing flew across the room and slammed into the cage again and again.

"Come on, ya palooka!" Meowth called out. "Keep fighting!"

Jessie threw a Poké Ball. "Arbok, use your Poison Sting!"

A purple cobra Pokémon slid out of the ball. It joined Weezing's attack, pummeling the force field with one sting after another.

Pikachu and Charizard continued to assault the force field around Moltres's cage, but it wasn't working.

Ash knew he needed more power. He held out two Poké Balls. Squirtle and Bulbasaur appeared in a flash of light.

"Help Pikachu and Charizard!" Ash commanded.

Squirtle fired a stream of water at the bars. Bulbasaur lashed at the bars with two vines that came out of the plant bulb on its back.

Ash watched as Pikachu, Charizard, Squirtle, and Bulbasaur bombarded the force field with water, fire, electricity, and vines. Then he noticed that Tracey looked suddenly afraid.

"The water and electricity blasts are creating two gases, hydrogen and oxygen," Tracey said. "If those two gases come into contact with Charizard's fire, there's going to be an —"

BOOM! An explosion rocked the cage around Moltres, blowing apart the force field and blasting a hole in the wall of the ship. Ash's Pokémon were blown back by the force of the blast.

Moltres stretched its long wings, finally freed.

"Maaaaaaw!" screeched the giant bird.

Moltres flew out of the broken cage.

"It's going to attack us!" Ash yelled. He ducked and held his arms over his head.

49

But Moltres flew right past Ash and the others. It stopped in front of the cage that held Zapdos.

"Maaaaaaw!" Moltres aimed a super fire blast at the cage — a blast larger than anything Charizard could muster.

There was another ear-splitting explosion, and the cage holding Zapdos collapsed. The Electric Pokémon was free!

Team Rocket ducked and covered their heads.

"I'd hate to get burned by their fire," Jessie said.

"I'd hate to get zapped by their lightning," James said.

"I'd hate to get hit by their large wings!" said Meowth.

Moltres and Zapdos flew out of the hole in the ship.

"They're free!" Misty said. "Maybe they'll return to their islands and everything will go back to normal again."

But Ash wasn't so sure it could be that easy. He ran to the window.

"Oh, no!" he cried. "They're attacking this ship!"

Moltres and Zapdos circled Lawrence

III's ship, squawking angrily. Moltres hit the ship with scorching streams of fire. Zapdos joined in with jolts of sizzling electricity.

Inside the ship, the lights blinked on and off. The ship rattled and shook.

A computer voice blared throughout the lab.

"Losing control. Losing control. Must make an emergency landing on Lightning Island."

Ash's stomach lurched as the ship plummeted to the ground with amazing speed.

Ash quickly recalled Squirtle, Bulbasaur, and Charizard. Then he grabbed Pikachu and waited for the worst.

Bam! The ship hit the ground with a sickening thud.

Then everything went black.

Chapter Eleven

Slowking's Challenge

Ash scrambled through the darkness to find the hole in the wall of the ship. A blast of wind in his face led him to it.

"Over here!" Ash called to his friends. "Let's get off this thing!"

Misty, Tracey, Melody, and Team Rocket followed Ash's voice to the opening. They helped one another climb out of the ship.

"We made it," Misty said, breathing a sigh of relief.

Ash surveyed the situation. The ship had crash-landed on a rocky peak. Half of it hung precariously over the rough seas, and part of it hung over a stone temple like the one on Fire Island. The ship teetered back and forth.

Up above, three Flying Pokémon circled the island. Moltres and Zapdos had been joined by a third Pokémon, one with blue feathers and a long, rippling tail. Ice crystals trailed behind the Pokémon as it flew.

"That must be Articuno," Ash exclaimed, "the one Lawrence III called the Titan of Ice!"

"They don't look happy," Tracey said. "We should probably try to get back to Shamouti Island — fast!"

"Right!" Ash agreed, but a thunderous noise kept him from speaking any further.

Moltres, Zapdos, and Articuno were bombarding the ship with swirling blasts of ice, lightning, and fire. The ship groaned as it broke into huge chunks.

Most of the ship splashed into the sea. Another part of it slammed down onto the stone temple.

"The sky is falling!" James cried, as heavy debris from the broken ship rained down on them.

Ash held Pikachu underneath him and threw himself on the ground. He covered his head with his hands.

A piece of metal clattered inches away from him. And then something else landed in front of them. A round, clear globe. Inside the globe, a golden light burned brightly.

Ash couldn't believe it. "It's the treasure of Lightning Island!" he cried excitedly. He tucked it safely inside his vest.

The rain of debris stopped. Ash stood up.

"Let's get out of here!" he yelled.

"What about that Lawrence III guy?" Tracey asked, looking back at the ship.

"He can take care of himself," Ash said.

Ash headed down toward the beach. There had to be some way to get off Lightning Island. The others followed closely behind.

As they ran, another danger came down from above.

Moltres blasted the island with fiery flames.

Zapdos zapped the island with jolts of electricity.

Articuno froze the island with an icy torrent.

"I wish we were blasting off right now!" Jessie complained.

Ash could see the shore in the distance. Then he saw a welcome sight.

"Maren!" Ash cried.

Their friend stood in her boat. "I figured you guys could use a lift," she said, smiling. "Luckily, I was able to fix the boat's rudder."

"You've got that right!" Ash said.

Ash and the others quickly climbed aboard. Team Rocket jumped into a life raft on the bottom deck.

"If this ship goes down, we'll be safe in here," James said.

"*Meowth!* I don't know if we'll ever be safe from those high-flying fiends," Meowth said, anxiously scanning the sky.

Maren steered the boat away from the shore.

The Legendary Pokémon aimed their attacks at the water. Suddenly, a large wave rose up behind the boat.

The wave lifted the boat higher than Ash thought possible. Then it slowly started to pull back.

"Hang on!" Maren cried.

Ash's stomach dropped as he looked down. How were they going to make it?

As if in answer to his thoughts, a gently spinning whirlpool rose up underneath them. Just as the wave dropped them, the whirpool picked them up.

"This is amazing," Tracey remarked. "I've never seen anything like it."

The whirlpool traveled in a straight line across the sea. Soon Shamouti Island loomed just ahead.

The spinning whirlpool began to get lower and lower. Then it tossed the boat onto the sandy shore.

As the boat slammed down, the life raft came loose — with Team Rocket inside. A gust of wind picked up the raft and sent it flying away from the island.

"I guess we're blasting off after all!" Team Rocket cried.

Ash climbed down onto the beach.

"Is everyone all right?" he asked.

"Pika!" Pikachu replied. Misty, Melody, Tracey, and Maren all nodded.

"What next?" Ash wondered aloud. He felt like he was on a roller-coaster ride that wouldn't stop.

"Now you must follow me," a deep voice said.

Ash spun around. His mouth dropped open.

A pink Pokémon stood in front of him. The Pokémon looked like Slowbro, but it walked on two legs. A crown made from the silver shell of a Shellder covered its head, and a ruffled collar circled its neck.

"Did you say something?" Ash asked. Meowth was the only talking Pokémon he knew.

"Follow me," the Pokémon repeated.

"That's Slowking," Melody whispered in Ash's ear. "Slowking guards the temple on Shamouti Island. It's an important part of our festival."

Ash and the others followed Slowking up stone steps. Soon they came to a temple made of slabs of rock. Ash thought it looked kind of like the temple on Fire Island, but this one was a little fancier. The stone hut had three windows inside. Seven tall pillars surrounded the hut.

Slowking walked up to the first window. Ash looked through it and could see that it gave a perfect view of Fire Island.

"Take the treasure, Ash," Slowking said.

"Put it there." The Pokémon pointed to a small stand in front of the window.

Ash took the two globes out of his jacket. One of the globes began to glow with red light. Ash placed this one in front of the window with a view of Fire Island.

The globe glowed brighter than before. Then it stopped.

"Now Lightning Island," Slowking said, walking to the third window. Ash could see Lightning Island through the opening. He put the second treasure on a stand in front of this window.

The treasure glowed with golden light, and then the light faded.

Slowking walked to the middle window. Ash paused.

"Uh, I only have two treasures," he said, a little embarassed.

Slowking gazed out the middle window. "We're one short," it said. "This is not good."

Ash followed Slowking's gaze. He could see Ice Island. A tall, thin mountain peak rose up in the center of the island. The three Legendary Bird Pokémon circled the peak, angrily fighting among themselves. Now they were shooting beams of fire, lightning, ice at one another. The beams looked like red, yellow, and blue lasers.

Suddenly, the birds turned and faced Shamouti Island, as if they knew they were being watched. They swiftly flew to Slow-king's temple, shooting red, yellow, and blue beams ahead of them.

Ash couldn't face another attack. He was tired of running. Tired of fighting.

Ash walked in front of the temple and held his hands out wide.

"Stop it!" he yelled as loud as he could. "Stop it right now!"

Ash's plea only angered the birds. They came together and focused their aim on him.

Fear rooted Ash to the spot. There was nowhere to run.

Ash cringed, waiting for the worst.

It didn't come.

A whirlpool rose from the water, just like the one that had safely carried their boat to Shamouti Island.

The spinning whirlpool created a wind that blew back Zapdos, Moltres, and Artic-uno.

Then a form emerged from the whirlpool. Ash had never seen anything like it.

The Pokémon was large, larger than even the Legendary Pokémon.

At first Ash thought it was a sea creature. It had smooth white skin, like a seal, and a flipperlike tail.

Then Ash noticed its wide wings and its curved beak. The Pokémon had a blue mask around its eyes, a blue belly, and blue ridges down its back.

Next to Ash, Slowking respectfully bowed its head.

"The Water's Great Guardian!" Slowking said, its voice filled with awe. "Lugia!"

Chapter Twelve

Lugia!

"It's just like the legend says," Melody said. "'The Water's Great Guardian shall arise to quell the fighting.'"

Lugia lifted its wings and hovered above the water. It let out a strange musical cry.

"The flute!" Melody gasped. "Lugia's cry matches the song I play at the festival!"

Lugia's blue eyes seemed to pierce through Ash, as though it wanted to tell him something.

But Lugia didn't have a chance. Moltres, Zapdos, and Articuno quickly recovered from being blown back, and now all three charged at Lugia.

Moltres aimed a red beam of fire energy at Lugia.

Zapdos aimed a golden beam of electric energy.

Articuno aimed a blue beam of ice energy at the Water's Great Guardian.

There was no way to dodge the beams. Ash watched as the blue ridges on Lugia's back retracted, leaving the Pokémon's back white and smooth.

Lugia lowered its head and gracefully dove into the water. The beams evaporated in midair.

"Good move," Ash said under his breath.

The water began to bubble and churn, and another whirlpool rose up. Ash could see Lugia's body inside the whirlpool.

This must be one of Lugia's attacks, Ash thought.

Articuno flew to the whirlpool and hurled a shower of ice crystals at the spinning funnel of water. In a flash, the whirlpool froze.

Lugia was trapped inside!

"Oh, no!" Ash cried.

The ice began to crack and break and then exploded into a million pieces. Lugia burst out of the icy trap, looking strong and confident.

But Moltres, Zapdos, and Articuno quickly surrounded Lugia. Each legendary bird sent out a whirlpool of energy.

The fire, electricity, and ice swirled around Lugia. A bubble appeared around its body. Ash guessed this was some kind of shield. At first, the attacks bounced off the bubble without doing any damage. But Moltres, Zapdos, and Articuno didn't give up.

Finally, the pounding, whirling pools of fire, electricity, and ice took their toll on Lugia. The protective bubble burst. From the shore of Shamouti Island, Ash could see the huge creature start to weaken. It was too weak to fly away, too weak to dive to safety.

Exhausted, Lugia fell from the sky. It splashed into the water below.

"Aaaaaaaaaaar!" Articuno swooped down and blasted the surface of the water with a strong ice beam.

Ash watched in horror as the surface of the sea became a crystal blanket of ice. The ice seemed to stretch for miles.

"Lugia is trapped!" said Tracey, who was watching the action with his binoculars.

The three Flying Pokémon gave a loud victory cry and continued their battle back on Ice Island.

Slowking sadly looked out over the frozen sea. "There is only one hope," it said. "Only the Chosen One can bring together the treasures to help the Water's Great Guardian."

"But the legend says that the song will fail!" Melody said. "It says the earth shall turn to ash. How can we help the Guardian if we don't even know who the real Chosen One is?"

Slowking repeated the words of the legend. "Though the Water's Great Guardian shall arise to quell the fighting, alone its song will fail. *Thus the earth shall turn to Ash,*" Slowking said.

Misty gasped. "It's right in the legend," she said. "'The earth shall turn to Ash!'" Misty turned to look directly at Ash. "Ash, the Chosen One really is you!"

"Me? It's really me?" Being the Chosen One had sounded kind of mysterious and exciting to Ash before. Now it seemed serious — *deadly* serious.

"Uh, I want to be a Pokémon Master more than anything," Ash said. "But do I really have to save the world?"

"You're the only one who matches the legend perfectly," Tracey said. "What do you say?"

"Well, right now I wish my mom had named me Bob instead of Ash," he answered.

Ash faced Melody. "You told me this would be easy!" he said accusingly.

Melody gave Ash a sympathetic look. "I'm sorry for dragging you into this," she said. "No one ever imagined the legend was real. We just acted out the legend at the festival because it was tradition. We were all just playing parts."

"I know," Ash said. He sighed. He couldn't just let the world go to pieces. He had to help. "So what happens now?"

Melody thought. "Well, the next part of the legend says, 'Climb to the shrine and right what is wrong and the world will be healed by the Guardian's song.' If the legend was right so far, then you need to find the third treasure and bring it here to the temple. Then you have to get Lugia to sing it's song — the one that sounds like this!"

Melody took her flute from a pouch attached to her belt. She raised the instrument to her lips and began to play.

Melody played the same beautiful tune she had played at the festival. The same tune that Lugia had sung. The song enchanted them all for a moment; Ash almost forgot about his worries.

The magical sound echoed all through the island. The sea began to glow with blue light under its icy covering.

The blue glow grew brighter. A round section of the ice started to melt and crack.

The water underneath started to spin — like a whirlpool!

Ash held his breath. Could it be Lugia?

It was! The giant Pokémon burst through the weakened ice and soared into the air. Behind it, the sky brightened, burning with an orange light.

Lugia swept down and landed on the beach near the temple.

"Behold," Lugia said. "The song has given me strength."

It took Ash a second to realize that Lugia's mouth was not moving. The Pokémon was sending its thoughts directly to Ash's mind.

From his friends' expressions, he could tell that they heard Lugia's thoughts, too.

"The song alone is not enough to restore the balance of nature, calm the storm, and bring harmony to these warring Pokémon," Lugia communicated.

"What do you mean?" Ash asked.

"When the treasures of Fire, Ice, and Lightning are placed together in the temple, my song shall harmonize with their powers and tame the beasts both above and below the sea." Lugia continued. "But this can come to pass only with the help of the Chosen One . . ."

"You are the One," Lugia said.

"What can I do that somebody else can't?" Ash asked.

"Only in the hands of the true Chosen One will the ice sphere glow like the others, its power awakened," Lugia explained.

Lugia nodded toward Ice Island. Moltres, Zapdos, and Articuno circled the island once again, launching angry attacks on one another.

"I have to go there?" Ash asked. He couldn't imagine it. First he'd have to somehow cross the ice. Then he'd have to avoid the angry Pokémon, climb up to the temple, and get the treasure. And if he did all that, he'd still have to get the treasure back to Shamouti Island. It seemed impossible!

"You are the only one who can save the planet," Lugia said. "It is up to you."

Pikachu ran to Ash's side and faced Lugia. The small Pokémon wore a look of pride and determination.

"I guess you're with me, huh, Pikachu?" Ash asked.

"Pika!"

Then three Poké Balls on Ash's belt began to rattle. The Poké Balls fell to the ground and opened. Charizard, Squirtle, and Bulbasaur appeared.

"You guys are with me, too?" Ash asked.

The Pokémon nodded.

Ash took a deep breath. With his Pokémon by his side, he just might make it.

He turned to Misty, Tracey, and Melody.

"I know I get carried away sometimes," Ash said. "I know I can mess things up, too. But this time I'm going to do it right."

"You mean . . ." Misty's voice trailed off.

"I'm going to get the last treasure!" Ash said. "I'm going to save the world!"

Chapter Thirteen

Team Rocket to the Rescue?

"**W**hy does Ash get all the cool parts?" Jessie asked as she watched Ash and his Pokémon begin to cross the icy ocean.

Jessie, James, and Meowth were stranded on a mountaintop above Slowking's temple. The life raft had landed there when the whirlpool tossed them ashore. They huddled together, trying to stay warm and dry as another storm kicked up.

James frowned. "You're right, Jess," he said. "Ash always gets to be the hero. And we always end up looking like zeroes!"

Meowth sadly hung its head. "It looks like we'll never get a chance to show what we can do," it said.

Then Jessie's face brightened. She pointed to the sky. "Maybe we're not out of this yet."

James and Meowth looked up. A helicopter was flying toward the island. It looked like it was having trouble. The copter zigged and zagged across the sky, barely staying in the air.

Then the helicopter started to dip. It sank farther and farther down and finally landed with a bump in the sand.

"*Meowth!* What's this?" asked the scratch cat Pokémon.

Team Rocket hid behind a rock and watched the helicopter. A door swung open, and a group of people climbed out, looking dazed.

They were Professor Oak, Professor Ivy, Ash's mom, and a helicopter pilot.

"Is everyone all right?" Professor Ivy asked.

Ash's mom and Professor Oak nodded. "Where are we?" Mrs. Ketchum asked.

"I'm pretty sure we're on Shamouti Island," said the pilot. "We may have to walk a little bit to find the village."

"This copter's certainly no use to us now," Professor Oak said, looking at the mangled aircraft.

Ash's mom pulled her coat tightly around her shoulders and shivered. "Let's hurry, then," she said. "I've got to make sure Ash is all right!"

They all followed the pilot off the beach. Jessie, James, and Meowth came out of hiding.

Jessie looked at the helicopter. Then she looked at the life raft. And then she smiled.

"Perfect!" she said. "This is just what we need!"

Meowth kicked the helicopter. "What are we supposed to do with this hunk of junk?" it asked.

"Leave it to me," Jessie said. Then she turned around and looked out at the ice. "Look out, Ash! We're coming to —"

"— steal Pikachu?" James asked.

Jessie scowled. "No, you nincompoop. This is our chance to be heroes. We're going to help Ash save the day!"

Chapter Fourteen

Journey to Ice Island

Ash tried to get to Ice Island as fast as he could. It wasn't easy. A foot of snow covered the slippery ice. Ash took one slow, plodding step after another.

"I feel more like the *Frozen* One than the *Chosen* One," Ash said, shivering. "We'll never get there in time."

"Pikachu," said Pikachu, pointing to a wrecked boat sticking out of the ice.

"How can that help us?" Ash asked. "The whole ocean is frozen over."

But Bulbasaur, Squirtle, and Charizard knew what to do. They took a flat side panel off the boat. Squirtle found a length of rope and tied it to one end of the panel.

Then Ash realized what they were doing. He and Pikachu hopped onto the panel. Bulbasaur, Squirtle, and Charizard picked up the ropes and pulled the panel across the ice and snow, like a sled.

"Thanks, guys!" Ash called to his friends. Now they zipped along easily.

A shadow covered them, and Ash looked up. Lugia flew overhead. The giant beast looked down at Ash and smiled.

"We can do this," Ash said under his breath. "We're going to make it!"

Ice Island loomed closer.

But they were too close. Moltres, Zapdos, and Articuno noticed their arrival. They stopped fighting one another and tore through the sky, headed right for Ash and Lugia.

Crack! Zap! Sizzle!

Ice beams, electric beams, and fire beams tore up the ice in front of them.

Moltres and Zapdos swooped down and aimed their attentions at the Pokémon. Moltres opened its beak and shot a river of fire down from the sky. Zapdos let loose with an electric charge that looked like a lightning bolt.

Pikachu and Charizard jumped into action. Pikachu quickly aimed a Thunderbolt at the oncoming attack by Zapdos. The two bolts of electricity met in the air and then fizzled out.

Charizard opened its mouth wide and aimed a burst of fire at Moltres's fire. The two streams of fire met and then exploded in the air.

Articuno attacked Lugia, blasting it with a frozen beam. A shimmering bubble appeared around Lugia, blocking the icy assault.

Zapdos joined in the attack on Lugia. The Electric and Flying Pokémon zoomed down at Lugia, planning to knock it out of the sky. Lugia countered by slamming into Zapdos, sending the Pokémon spiraling away.

Moltres and Articuno cried angrily, then swooped down at Lugia. The Water's Great Guardian had no choice but to try to dodge them. It flew out over the ice, away from the island.

Ash knew Lugia had provided them with a distraction — even for a short time. All he had to do was get to the temple.

Ash stared out at the ice in front of him,

his hopes dashed. During the battle, the ice, fire, and electric attacks had ripped into the ice. Now big chunks of ice littered the path to the island. There was no way to cross.

Ash and Pikachu looked at each other, both thinking the same thing.

"I guess it ends here," Ash said sadly.

"Not so fast, Ash!" a familiar voice cried.

Ash spun around. Behind him, Jessie, James, and Meowth were riding a life raft powered by a helicopter propeller. The raft floated in the air like some kind of hovercraft.

"If that kid thinks we're here for trouble . . ." Jessie said.

". . . we're certainly going to burst *his* bubble!" James said. Jessie and James launched into a new motto.

"Instead of causing tribulation,
we're undergoing transformation!
Though it's way outside of our usual range,
we're going to do something nice for a change!
Jessie!
James!
Up till now Team Rocket's been quite un-scrupulous!

Being good guys for once would be su-perdupulous!"

"That's right!" finished Meowth.

Ash couldn't believe what he was hearing. "Team Rocket?" he asked. "Why do you want to help me?"

"If the whole world goes up in smoke . . ." James said.

". . . us bad guys won't have anything to be bad about!" Jessie finished.

Meowth rolled its eyes. "Things are going to get *really* bad if we don't get to Ice Island!"

Ash realized with surprise that he believed them. Besides, he didn't have a choice.

"Let's go!" Ash yelled. He jumped onto the hovering life raft, and his Pokémon followed.

Jessie steered the craft over the chunks of ice. Ash saw some steps up ahead that led inside a cave.

"In there!" Ash said.

Jessie maneuvered the raft through the winding cave. The walls around them were covered with smooth, glassy ice. Icicles hung from the roof.

The raft stopped right in front of the stone statue of Articuno. The bird's mouth was open, and there was something inside.

Ash reached in and touched the treasure. It was a clear globe, like all the others. But a blue light glowed in this one.

Ash yanked the globe out of the statue's mouth.

"I did it!" he cried. "I got the third treasure!"

"Yahoo!" yelled Jessie and James. They high-fived each other.

Meowth fidgeted nervously.

"This is no time to celebrate," Meowth said. "Those angry birds won't be gone for long. Let's pull out of here pronto."

"Right," said Ash. He put the treasure inside his jacket.

Ash, Pikachu, and Team Rocket raced to get to the raft. As soon as they got outside, a piercing cry told them they were too late.

"*Aaaaaaaaaaaaaw!*" Articuno shot a blue ice beam right at them. They had to dodge out of the way to escape it.

Then Moltres and Zapdos dove down and attacked them with red fire and gold electric beams. They dodged the attacks, but the beams hit the hovering raft instead, blowing it to pieces.

Ash stared at the ruined raft, panic growing inside him. There was no way off the island now.

"Pika!" Pikachu raced up a steep incline and stopped on a rocky ledge. The yellow Pokémon looked up at the sky.

Ash looked, too.

Lugia!

The white Pokémon landed on the ledge. Ash put Bulbasaur, Squirtle, and Charizard back in their Poké Balls. Then he ran up to meet Lugia.

"Did you get the treasure?" Lugia's deep psychic voice boomed in Ash's head.

"Of course!" Ash said.

Lugia nodded. "Get on."

Pikachu and Ash hopped on Lugia's back. The creature spread its giant wings and started to lift off.

"Wait for us!" Team Rocket called behind them. They grabbed onto Lugia's leg just in time.

Lugia soared through the sky, over the ice-covered sea. From his perch, Ash could see the thousands of Pokémon crossing the ice, trying to get to Shamouti Island. It was an amazing sight.

"*Zaaaaaaaaaaaaaaaw!*" Zapdos's screeching reminded him that they were still in danger. The Electric Pokémon was catching up.

Lugia tried to fly faster, but it was weighted down with its passengers.

Team Rocket knew why Lugia was slowing down. Jessie, James, and Meowth looked at one another.

"We're dragging them down," Jessie said. "The three of us are too heavy!"

Behind them, the Legendary Pokémon were getting closer.

"What do we do, Jess?" James asked.

Jessie looked down at the frozen sea.

"We can be zeroes," Jessie said.

James nodded. "Or we can be heroes."

"Let's do it!" Meowth cried. "It's our turn to save the day!"

Jessie, James, and Meowth let go of Lugia's leg. They held hands, forming a circle.

"Looks like Team Rocket's blasting off for gooood!" they yelled.

Ash heard them. "Team Rocket!" he cried, shocked.

The three Pokémon thieves spiraled down to the sea until Ash couldn't see them anymore.

Ash turned to Pikachu. "I guess they really did come to rescue us," he said a little sadly.

With the extra weight gone, Lugia picked up speed. Ash looked back. Moltres, Zapdos, and Articuno were too far away to catch up any time soon.

"We're going to do it!" Ash said. "We're going to get that third treasure to Slowking. We're going to save the world!"

"Pikachuuuuuu!!" Pikachu let out a panicked scream.

"What is it, Pikachu?"

Then Ash saw them. Two huge metal triangles whizzed through the air. The triangles were heading right for Lugia.

Ash recognized them. They looked like the diamond-shaped hoops that had trapped Zapdos.

"It's Stelthius!" Ash cried, as the horrible truth hit him. "Lawrence III is trying to capture Lugia!"

Chapter Fifteen

The End of Lugia?

Lawrence III's traps darted around Lugia's body. The giant Pokémon tried to speed past them.

Ash craned his neck. Down below, Lawrence III's battered ship stuck out of the water. Although much of the ship's equipment had been damaged in the crash, Lawrence III managed to get the traps working. The metal doors of the ship were open, waiting to receive their prize.

"Lugia!" Ash cried out. "Destroy the ship, and the traps will be useless!"

Lugia didn't respond but made a sharp turn in the sky and faced the ship.

Lugia opened its huge beak. A golden

ball of glowing light poured out of its mouth. The golden light hurtled through the air and then slammed into the metal ship.

"Maaaaaaaaaw!"

"Zaaaaaaaaaaw!"

"Aaaaaaaaaaar!"

The three legendary birds had caught up with them. They frantically flew in circles, as if they weren't sure what to attack first: Lugia or Lawrence III's ship.

Lugia didn't hesitate. It opened its mouth again, shooting another golden ball of light. The powerful beam swiped Moltres, Zapdos, and Articuno, sending them crashing into the ice. Then it hit its target.

Boom! An explosion rocked Lawrence III's ship.

"All right, Lugia!" Ash yelled.

"Pikachu!" Pikachu warned.

Lugia had destroyed the ship, but it was too late. The traps had done their job. They pinned Lugia's wings to its body, making it impossible for the Pokémon to fly.

Then Ash heard Lugia's voice inside his head.

"I have failed," Lugia said sadly.

Then the Pokémon plunged to the sea

with Ash and Pikachu still on its back. Ash gripped Pikachu tightly.

Lugia crashed through the ice, sinking into the cold, cold water. Ash let go of Lugia and kicked with all his might, trying to get to the surface.

Weak light shimmered through the surface of the water. Ash's lungs seemed like they would burst as he struggled to get to the surface.

Then his world went dark.

The next thing he saw was Misty's face. His friend swam alongside him, looking concerned. Ash felt a thick rope around his waist.

"You're okay, Ash," Misty said. "Tracey is pulling you in. We already got Pikachu to safety."

"Lugia?" Ash said weakly.

Misty's face clouded. "There's no sign of Lugia anywhere."

Ash wanted to go back, to swim back to the icy ocean and find Lugia. But he had no strength.

And the weather was getting worse. Jagged bolts of lightning lit up the sky. Dark tornado funnels careened across the surface of the water. Icy raindrops fell from the sky.

Tracey pulled Ash out of the water and onto the wet sand. Ash lay on his back, exhausted. He couldn't move. Couldn't help Lugia.

Lugia didn't fail, Ash thought. *I'm the one who failed. I was supposed to be the Chosen One, but I blew it.*

Then Ash felt something move inside his jacket.

And he remembered.

"The third treasure," Ash said weakly. "I've got to get it to the temple." This wasn't over yet!

Ash tried to stand up, but his legs buckled underneath him. Misty wrapped an arm around his waist.

"I've got to do this," Ash told Misty.

Misty nodded. She helped Ash up the steps to the ancient temple. Tracey and Pikachu followed behind.

Forceful gusts of winds pushed them back with each step. But Ash didn't stop. Step by step, he made his way to the temple.

Slowking and Melody waited at the top.

Ash

pocket.

"You are ..third treasure out of his
king said.

Ash let go of Misty ...

his own. He took a shaky ...ne." Slow-
temple.

Slowking pointed to the middle wi...
Through the opening, Ash could see Ice Island. Lawrence III's ruined ship was scat-
tered across the ice-covered water. And the
three Legendary Pokémon lay still, their
bodies bruised and battered. Lugia was
nowhere to be seen.

Ash put the treasure on the stand in
front of the window. Then he stepped back.

Nothing happened.

Ash wanted to cry. Had he gone through
all this for nothing?

And then, slowly, the three globes began
to glow.

Chapter Sixteen

The Legend Comes to Pass

Red light shone from the Fire Island treasure.

Yellow light shone from the Lightning Island treasure.

And blue light shone from the Ice Island treasure.

Ash watched, breathless, as the three colors of light converged in the center of the temple and turned into a beautiful shade of green. The light exploded from all sides of the temple, melting the snow on the ground in an instant.

Then the shimmering green light became almost liquid. It poured across the floor of the temple like honey, then rose up each of the seven pillars.

Melody stepped forward, her flute in her hands.

"According to the legend, 'the world will be healed by the Guardian's song,'" Melody said. "The song unlocks the power of the three treasures and will restore the balance of nature. The storm will end, and the legendary birds will be at peace. Lugia may not be able to sing its melody, but I can still play its song on my flute!" She began to play the tune from the festival.

Each time Melody played a note, a pillar gleamed with green light in response. As the beautiful notes filled the air, the weather grew calmer and calmer. The wind died down. The rain stopped. The underwater current known as the Beast of the Sea rose like a tornado into the sky and disappeared. The dark clouds parted, revealing a beautiful blue sky and shining sun behind them.

At the same time, the pillars began to glow more brightly, sending a soft blanket of light across the icy ocean and Shamouti Island. Whatever the light touched became whole and new again.

The ice gently melted away.

The three legendary birds began to stir. They opened their eyes and moved their majestic wings.

Tropical flowers appeared under the melting snow, exploding in a brilliant blaze of color.

Moltres, Zapdos, and Articuno rose up and flew in circles in the sky. But this time, their flight was happy and beautiful, instead of filled with anger.

Moltres flew back to its perch on Fire Island. Zapdos returned to Lightning Island. Articuno landed on Ice Island.

"It is over," Slowking said. "The Beast of the Sea has been tamed. The balance of nature has been restored."

The music of the flute ended. The green light faded from the pillars.

Ash gazed out at the three islands, relieved that the world was no longer in danger. But still, he couldn't be happy. Lugia was gone.

"*Pikachu,*" Pikachu said sadly. The Electric Pokémon felt the same way.

"Ash, look!" Misty cried out.

A bright blue whirlpool rose out of the ocean. The whirlpool spun across the water and then stopped in front of the temple.

Water splashed all over Ash as a large white Pokémon rocketed out of the whirlpool and flew to the temple.

"Lugia!" Ash cried happily.

Chapter Seventeen

One Last Ride

"**C**limb on," Lugia said.

Ash and Pikachu hopped on Lugia's back. The great Guardian soared through the sky. The powers of the song and the treasures had healed Lugia as well.

The sun warmed Ash's back, drying his soggy clothes. Below them, the blue ocean water glittered in the sunlight.

"Pika!" Pikachu said happily.

Ash smiled at the Pokémon. Their last flight on Lugia's back was filled with danger. But this was the ride of a lifetime.

In the distance, Ash could see thousands of Pokémon walking, swimming, and flying away from Shamouti Island. They knew everything was going to be all right.

Lugia dipped and twirled in the sky. The Pokémon didn't say anything, but Ash knew that part of the happy, joyous energy he was feeling was coming from Lugia.

Ash could have flown all day, but Lugia returned to Shamouti Island and stopped in front of the temple. Ash and Pikachu climbed down.

Lugia's voice boomed in Ash's head. "The Beast of the Sea has been tamed," Lugia said. "The fate of the world could not have been in better hands."

Lugia flew off of the island and then dove back into the sea. Ash watched as the last drops of water splashed down to the surface, and then he turned around.

Melody, Misty, and Tracey ran up to him.

"You did it, Ash!" Misty said proudly.

"You really are the Chosen One," Melody added.

"We did it together," Ash said.

Then a tired voice interrupted them.

"It figures. We do all the work, and Ash gets all the credit," Jessie said.

"Team Rocket!" Ash cried. Jessie, James, and Meowth climbed the steps, looking scraggly and exhausted. Normally, he would be angry just at the sight of them, but part of him was relieved. They had saved him, after all.

"Thanks for saving the world, Ash," James said. "Now we can go back to stealing Pokémon."

"You guys will never change," Misty said. "Aren't you tired of causing trouble?"

Jessie, James, and Meowth looked over the island, which was now covered with beautiful flowers. Then they looked at one another and smiled.

"*Meowth!* We'll be after Pikachu again," Meowth said. "But maybe we'll take a little rest first!"

Ash couldn't help smiling. Then he remembered something.

"What should we do about Lawrence III?" Ash asked his friends.

"His ship is destroyed," Tracey pointed out. "I don't think he'd be foolish enough to try this again."

Ash looked out at the three islands,

which were now peaceful and calm. He hoped Tracey was right.

"Ash! Ash!"

Ash spun around. He couldn't believe it. His mom was walking down the mountain! Professor Oak and Professor Ivy were behind her.

"The ocean current is back to normal," Professor Oak said. "The dangerous weather should be over."

Ash's mom ran up and hugged her son tightly. "I was watching you, Ash!" she said. "How could you do something so dangerous?"

"But Ash saved the world," Misty said.

"He may have saved the world, but he took reckless chances," Mrs. Ketchum said. "What's a world without you in it?"

Ash's mom hugged him again. He blushed.

Mrs. Ketchum looked her son in the eyes. "Ash, what do you want to do with your life?"

Ash didn't hesitate. "I want to become a Pokémon Master!" he said confidently.

"Then do it," his mom replied. "But don't

be so careless. And maybe next time you can try saving the world a little closer to home."

"*Pikachu!*" Pikachu agreed.

"You're right," Ash said.

Melody hugged him now. "You'll be a great Pokémon Master, Ash," she said. "I know it."

"He will as long as he has us to help him!" Misty said.

Ash blushed again. Then he turned away and gazed out over the water. He had wanted to be a Pokémon Master since he was a little kid. But he wasn't a little kid anymore. He had learned a lot on his Pokémon journey. Now it was time to use what he'd learned.

Ash turned back to his mom and his friends. Pikachu jumped into his arms.

"I'm going to make you all proud," Ash told them. "I'm going to be the best Pokémon Master ever!"

Somewhere deep in the ocean, Lugia heard Ash's words.

And smiled.